The Jar of Fools

The Jar of Fools

Eight Hanukkah Stories from Chelm

by
Eric A.
Kimmel

illustrated by
Mordicai
Gerstein

SCHOLASTIC INC.

New York Toronto London Auckland Sydney
Mexico City New Delhi Hong Kong

ISBN 0-439-30034-7

A version of "Sweeter Than Honey, Purer Than Oil" was previously published in
Spider: The Magazine for Children.

A version of "The Soul of the Menorah" was published in *Cricket Magazine.*

Text copyright © 2000 by Eric A. Kimmel.
Illustrations copyright © 2000 by Mordicai Gerstein. All rights reserved.
Published by Scholastic Inc., 555 Broadway, New York, NY 10012,
by arrangement with Holiday House, Inc.
SCHOLASTIC and associated logos are trademarks and/or registered
trademarks of Scholastic Inc.

12 11 10 9 8 7 6 5 4 3 2 1   1 2 3 4 5 6/0

Printed in the U.S.A.   14

First Scholastic printing, November 2001

The art work was prepared with ink drawings on oil paint.

The hand lettering on the half-title pages is Bernard Maisner.

The text typeface is Stempel Scneidler, chosen for its Chelmian upside-down
question marks.

In memory of
Mort Malter
E. A. K.

For Risa,
because I love to
hear you laugh
M. G.

Contents

THE JAR OF FOOLS

Everyone knows that Chelm is a town of fools. Or so it is said. The question is, if the people of Chelm are truly as foolish as everyone believes they are, how did so many fools come to be gathered in one place? And why is that place Chelm?

According to one legend, it happened a long time ago, just after Adam and Eve left the Garden of Eden.

God looked down from heaven. He saw that the number of human beings in the world was growing. Soon they would spread all over the earth. All the new human beings who were going to be born would need souls.

God made a great kettle in the sky. Using the Big Dipper as a spoon and the Little Dipper as a ladle, He mixed up a huge number of souls. Some of these souls liked to quarrel. Others were peaceful.

God looked at the souls He had made and said, "It is not good for all the quarrelsome souls to be in one place and all the peaceful souls to be in another. If that were to happen, the quarrelsome nations would have no one to temper their aggression. The peaceful nations would have no one to defend them. It is better for these souls to be distributed evenly. Every country would then have citizens who value peace as well as others capable of waging war."

God put the quarrelsome souls in one jar and the peaceful souls in another. He gave each jar to an angel, telling them to spread the souls over the earth, making sure there were not too many of either kind in one place or too few in another. The angels did as God commanded. God looked down and saw that it was good.

God took the Big Dipper and the Little Dipper in hand again and mixed up another batch of souls. Some were honest, and some were dishonest. God looked at the souls and said, "It is not good for all these souls to be in one place either. Justice and honor cannot thrive in a nation where everyone is a scoundrel. There must be honest folk to control the dishonest ones. Only then will honor and justice be valued."

God put the honest souls into one jar and the dishonest souls into another. He handed each jar to an angel, telling them to spread the souls throughout the world. The angels did as God commanded. God looked down and saw that it was good.

God filled up the kettle a third time. He made another batch of souls. Some were wise and some were foolish. God looked at the souls He made and said, "It is not good for all the wise people and all the foolish people to be in one place. The wise would become so clever that nobody would be able to understand them. The fools

would tumble blindly into folly. Let both kinds of souls be distributed evenly across the earth, as was done with the others."

God put the wise souls into one jar and the foolish souls into another. He handed each jar to an angel, saying, "Take these souls and distribute them evenly. Let there not be too many of either kind in one place or too few in another."

The first angel took the jar containing the wise souls and spread them over the earth. That is why there are wise people in every family, in every town, in every nation. However, the angel carrying the jar with the foolish souls was a butterfingers. He was flying along when the jar slipped from his hands. It fell to the ground and shattered. That is how all the truly foolish souls came to be in one place.

That place is Chelm.

However, there is another version of this story. According to that version, the jar the angel dropped was not the one containing foolish souls at all, but the one filled with wise souls.

That is how the people of Chelm came to be so wise that nobody else understands them. Everybody regards them as fools.

But are they really? No one can say, for no one knows which version of the story is true.

However, that's how they tell it in Chelm.

How They Play Dreidel in Chelm

Everybody knows about dreidels. A dreidel is a four-sided top with one Hebrew letter on each side. The letters are *nun, gimel, heh,* and *shin.* They stand for the Hebrew words *Nes Gadol Haya Sham.* In English that means, *A Great Miracle Happened There.*

The sages of Chelm were playing dreidel one Hanukkah evening when the oldest, Motke Fool, said, "I think this dreidel has too many letters."

"How can a dreidel have too many letters?" the others asked. "For thousands of years dreidels have had the same four letters: *nun, gimel, heh,* and *shin.* They remind us of the miracle of Hanukkah."

"I still think four letters are too many. We don't need all of them," said Motke.

"Which ones would you get rid of?"

"I'd get rid of the letter *shin,*" said Motke. "What does it stand

for? *Sham*, which means *There*. Why do we need this letter? We know the miracle happened there, in the land of Israel. It didn't happen *here*, in Chelm. Nothing ever happens in Chelm."

"You're right," the sages agreed. They took a bottle of ink and blotted out the letter *shin*.

"I know another letter we can get rid of," said Simon Goose. "Consider *heh*. What does it stand for? *Haya*, which means *Happened*. Obviously the miracle happened. If it didn't happen, we wouldn't be celebrating Hanukkah. Today would just be an ordinary day."

"That's true," the sages agreed as they blotted out the letter *heh*.

Then Berel Dunce piped up. "I know another letter we can do without!"

"Which one?"

"*Gimel*. It stands for *Gadol,* meaning *Great*. Why do we need to say 'a *great* miracle'? Aren't all miracles great? Who ever heard of an ordinary miracle?"

"What wisdom!" the sages exclaimed as they blotted out the letter *gimel*.

"Wait! We're not done," said Feivel Bonehead. "Look at *nun*. What does it stand for? *Nes,* which means *Miracle*. I ask you, when a tiny band of Jews, no braver or smarter than we are, defeats a great nation like the mighty Greeks of old, what do you call it?"

"A miracle!"

"Of course! Everybody knows that. We don't need some silly letter to remind us."

So the sages of Chelm took the bottle of ink and blotted out the remaining letter, *nun.*

Ever since that time dreidels in Chelm have been made without letters. The four sides are blank.

So how do they play the dreidel game? The same way everyone else plays it, with dreidels, coins, nuts, candies.

Except in Chelm—strange to say—whenever they play dreidel, everyone always wins.

Sweeter than Honey, Purer than Oil

One afternoon Esther Goose said to her son, "Velvel, tonight our cousins are coming over for Hanukkah. I don't have enough chicken fat to cook the latkes. Here is a zloty. Be a good boy. Go to the market and buy a pound of chicken fat for me. Hurry. The market will close soon."

Velvel took the zloty and started out the door.

"Velvel, wait!" his mother called after him. "There is chicken fat and there is chicken fat. Don't let anyone cheat you. Be sure to buy only the best."

"Don't worry, Mama," Velvel called back, "I'll remember. Only the best."

Velvel ran to the market. He stopped at the butcher's stall. "Do you have chicken fat?" he asked.

The butcher laughed. "Do I have chicken fat? Of course I have chicken fat! How could I call myself a butcher and not have chicken fat?"

"Ah, but what kind of chicken fat is it?"

"What kind? The best! My chicken fat is as smooth as butter."

Velvel began to think. *If chicken fat is as smooth as butter, then butter must be better than chicken fat. Mama said to buy only the best. I'll buy butter.*

"Never mind," he told the butcher. He ran to the dairyman's stall.

"Do you have any butter?" he asked the dairyman.

"Do I have butter? Of course I have butter! My butter is as sweet as honey."

If butter is as sweet as honey, then honey must be better than butter. I'll buy honey, thought Velvel.

"Never mind," he told the dairyman. He ran to the honey seller's booth.

"Do you have any honey?" he asked the honey seller.

"Do I have honey? Of course I have honey! My honey is as clear as oil."

Velvel thought, *If honey is as clear as oil, then oil must be better than honey. I'll buy oil.*

"Never mind," Velvel said. He ran to the oil seller's shop.

"Do you have any oil?" he asked the oil seller.

"Of course I have oil! The very best! My oil is as pure as water."

Aha! thought Velvel. *If oil is as pure as water, then water must be better than oil. Why should I waste Mama's zloty? I can get water for free.*

"Never mind," Velvel said. He ran to the town pump just as the

farmer to come through town. Motke put them on. He was very pleased. Now he could walk around Chelm all day without muddying his golden slippers. However, another problem appeared.

"The boots keep out the mud, but they also hide the slippers."

Motke was right. If nobody could see the slippers, nobody would know how wise he was. If nobody knew how wise he was, what was the point in wearing them?

The sages of Chelm had to start thinking again. After a while Simon Goose spoke up. "The boots are made of felt. Felt isn't hard to cut. We'll cut holes in the boots. Then the golden slippers can show through."

Simon took the boots back to his tailor shop and cut out pretty patterns of menorahs and dreidels in honor of Hanukkah.

When Motke put the boots back on, the golden slippers shined through the cutout patterns. Everyone could see the slippers, and the clumsy boots themselves were now beautifully decorated with golden menorahs and dreidels.

Motke went for a walk. He soon returned, completely discouraged.

"These boots don't work. It's the same problem. Mud comes through the holes and covers the slippers."

What to do?

"I know!" said Stupid Shmelke, the town beggar. "My boots are always full of holes. Do I worry? No! I stuff them with straw. The straw keeps out the mud and my feet stay dry."

Now that was thinking! The sages of Chelm stuffed some straw into Motke's boots. Motke put them on and went for another walk. Again he returned, shaking his head.

"It still doesn't work. The straw keeps the mud out, but it also fills the holes so nobody can see the slippers."

This was becoming a serious problem. Even so, the sages of Chelm never despaired. They had faith that they would find an answer if they thought hard enough. After all, why else had God given them brains?

"Maybe we should start over," said Feivel Bonehead. "Let's forget the slippers. We'll find some other way to honor Motke. What if he wore a special hat?"

Nobody cared for that idea. Motke liked the slippers, and Berel had worked hard to make them.

"I know!" said Stupid Shmelke. "Motke can keep the slippers, but why must he wear them on his feet? Couldn't he wear them someplace else where they wouldn't get muddy and everyone could see them?"

"Where?"

"He could wear them on his hands."

"But I need to use my hands," said Motke. "How can I pick anything up if my hands are inside a pair of slippers?"

"You could tie them on a string and hang them around your neck," Esther Goose suggested.

"That's a stupid idea. My beard would cover them."

"Well, then stick them on your ears!" snapped Esther.

Ah! Now that was a solution! Motke could wear the slippers on his ears. The slippers would keep his ears warm, everyone would be able to see them, and they wouldn't get covered with mud.

Ever since that day people honored as Knights of the Golden Slippers have the privilege of wearing a pair of slippers on their ears for an entire year.

That's why it is always easy to identify Chelm's wisest, most honored, and distinguished citizen. He's the one who walks around town with a pair of slippers on his ears.

Silent Samson, the Maccabee

Everyone knows about Judah Maccabee and his heroic brothers. There would be no Hanukkah without them. Long ago, in ancient times, the Maccabees defeated the Greeks and saved the Jewish people.

Chelm had a Maccabee, too. His name was Silent Samson. Unlike Judah and his heroic brothers, Silent Samson did not wear armor or carry a sword. But he saved his people all the same. Had it not been for Silent Samson, Chelm would have been destroyed. Every year, throughout the eight nights of Hanukkah, the people of Chelm tell his story.

Four hundred years ago an army of Cossacks overran Poland. The Cossacks were as cruel as Amalek in the Bible. They burned towns and cities by the score. They murdered people like flies. Death and destruction followed wherever they went.

A Cossack army led by the famous Hetman Chmielnitski arrived at the gates of Chelm. The soldiers guarding the walls had run away during the night. Chelm was defenseless. The townspeople had no choice but to open the gates.

The Cossacks marched into Chelm. They were in a merry mood, eager for fun.

"Let's find two blind men and make them fight with clubs!"

"Let's find some people who can't walk and make them race!"

"Let's cut off some heads and play ninepins!"

The Cossacks forced the people of Chelm to line up in the town square. They looked them over one by one as they tried to decide what to do with them. The people of Chelm shook with fear. Some began to weep. Others begged for mercy. The Cossacks laughed.

Only one person did not cringe before the Cossacks. His real name has been forgotten. Everyone called him Silent Samson because he was big and strong, like Samson in the Bible. He was silent because he could not speak. Silent Samson had lost his hearing when he was a baby. He had never learned to talk. He communicated by making signs with his hands. Only his daughter could understand them. She interpreted for her father.

Silent Samson was not afraid of anyone. He stood calmly, watching the Cossacks, his muscular arms folded across his broad chest.

"Here's a stout fellow! We'll have some fun with him." One of the Cossacks grabbed Silent Samson's beard. Silent Samson picked him up and tossed him over his head. The Cossacks gasped to see their comrade flying through the air like a rag doll. Then they laughed.

"Here's the one we want! We'll make him sorry he was ever born."

Silent Samson turned to his daughter. He made signs with his hands. His daughter signed back.

"What are you doing?" the Cossacks asked.

"My father can't talk. That is why he is called Silent Samson," the girl explained. "We speak to each other with signs."

The Cossacks started arguing. "What shall we do with this fellow?"

"Sew him in a sack and throw him in the river!"

"Tie him to a tree and use him for target practice!"

"Spread hot coals on the ground. Make him dance on them barefoot!"

"We've done all that before," said Hetman Chmielnitski, the Cossack chief. "I want some different entertainment. Our minds need a challenge. Let's have a debate."

"A debate?" the Cossacks asked one another. "Silent Samson can't talk. How can he debate anything?"

"He can talk with his hands. We'll have a silent debate. A debate with signs instead of words."

The Cossacks agreed that this would be good sport.

Hetman Chmielnitski pointed to one of his colonels. "Here is Ataman Krivo, the cleverest of my officers. He can read and write. He has studied at the famous University of Krakow. He can speak

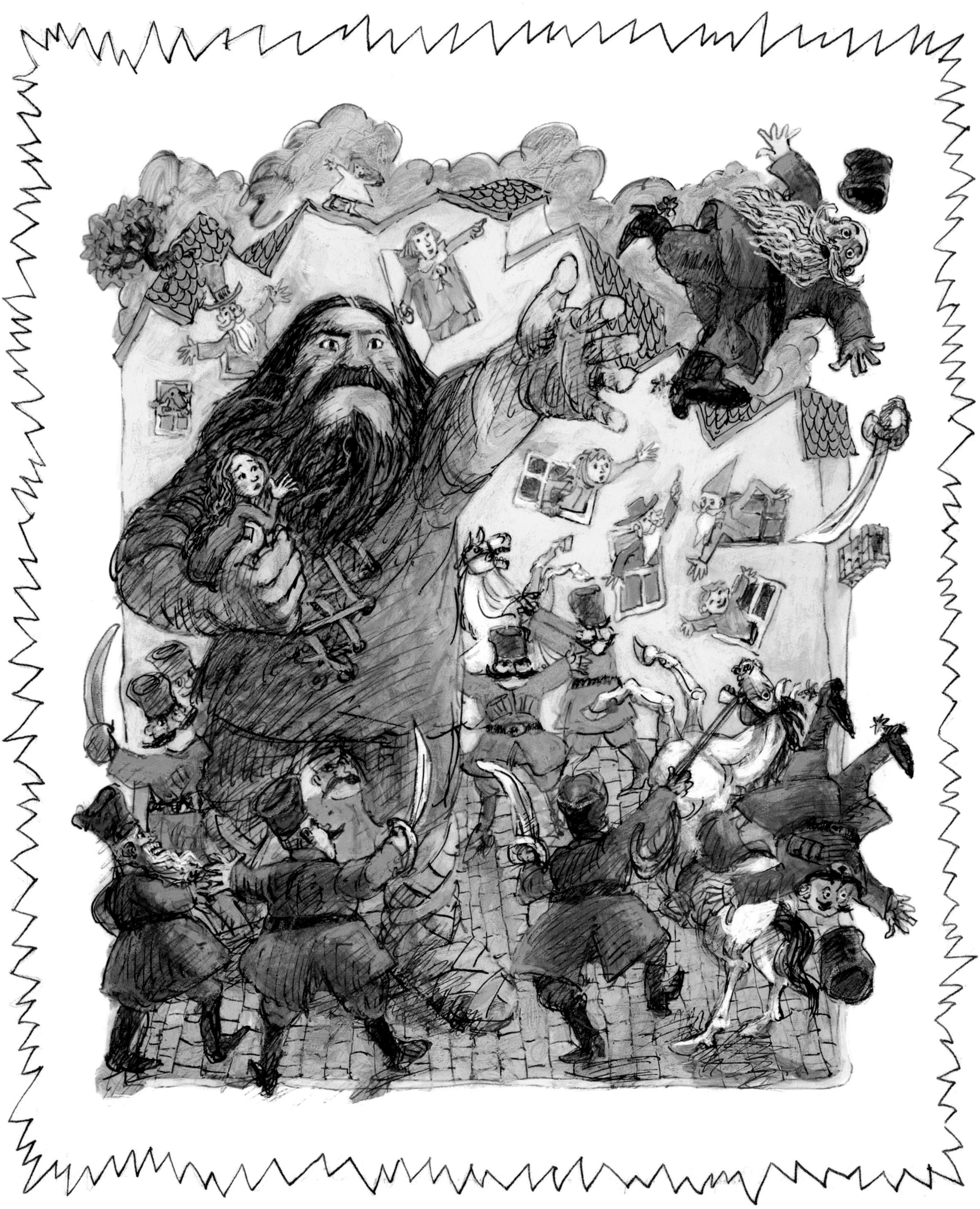

Latin and Greek. Why, he has even been known to read books!"

Ataman Krivo beamed with pride.

The other Cossacks nodded their heads as the hetman continued. "Ataman Krivo will represent us in the debate. The debate will be conducted entirely without words. At the end I will decide who wins. If it is Silent Samson, we will leave Chelm as we found it. If it is Ataman Krivo, the town and everything in it belongs to us, to do with as we like."

The people of Chelm had no choice but to agree to these terms. A table spread with bread, wine, and cheese was set up in the town square. Hetman Chmielnitski sat down. He filled his goblet with wine and motioned for the debate to begin.

Ataman Krivo approached Silent Samson. He held up both hands, with his two index fingers crossed.

Silent Samson did not hesitate. He held out his hand with his index and little finger pointed straight forward.

Ataman Krivo frowned. The Cossacks and townspeople began to murmur. What did this mean? Ataman Krivo suddenly raised his right hand with all five fingers outstretched.

Silent Samson raised his fist.

Ataman Krivo hesitated. He turned to the table and filled a goblet with wine. He held it out to Silent Samson.

Silent Samson picked up a piece of cheese. He offered it to Ataman Krivo.

Ataman Krivo gave up. "Silent Samson has beaten me," he said. "How can a man who can't talk defeat a graduate of the University of Krakow?" cried Hetman Chmielnitski.

"I will explain," said Ataman Krivo. "I began by holding up two crossed fingers, meaning, 'Your people and mine have been enemies since the world began.' Silent Samson answered by pointing two fingers at me as if to say, 'That is not true. In the beginning there were only two people, Adam and Eve. All the nations of the earth are their children. We all belong to one family. Why can't we live in peace?'"

"That is true," Hetman Chmielnitski agreed. "It says so in the Bible." The Cossacks nodded their heads.

Ataman Krivo continued. "I tried another argument. I held up my hand with fingers outstretched as if to say, 'Because of their sins, God exiled your forefathers from their land and scattered them throughout the world.' Silent Samson replied by holding up his fist. He meant to say, 'That is true. But remember that the God Who punishes sins also forgives them. One day He will gather us from the four corners of the earth, to be one nation again.' What could I say to that? These very words were spoken by the prophets in the Bible."

"If the Bible says so, it must be true," the Cossacks agreed.

"I made one last effort," Ataman Krivo went on. "I took a goblet of wine from the table and held it out to Silent Samson. I meant to say, 'It will be a long time before that happens. The sins of your people are as red as blood, as red as this wine.'"

"Yes!" the Cossacks shouted. "What did he say to that?"

"He held out the cheese, meaning 'Do we burn down cities? Do we kill people for sport? We may not be perfect, but compared to yours, our sins are as white as this cheese. Beware, Cossacks! If you do not change your ways, God will turn His face from you. He will deliver you into the hands of your enemies. You will vanish from the earth like the nations of old, and none will mourn your passing.'"

The Cossacks looked at one another. Suddenly they felt frightened and ashamed. One by one they sheathed their swords. They put away their muskets and pistols. Without a word they mounted their horses and rode out through the gates of Chelm, never to return.

There was great rejoicing in Chelm that night. However, one question remained. How was Silent Samson able to speak so eloquently? He had never been to school. He could not read or write.

The sages of Chelm asked Silent Samson's daughter to ask her father how he had thought of such brilliant arguments. The girl signed to Silent Sampson. He signed back. She began to laugh.

"What did he say?" the people of Chelm asked.

"My father says, 'Answering that ignorant Cossack was easy. When he crossed his fingers, I knew what he was up to. He was trying to put some evil spell on me. I pointed two fingers at him. He knew what I meant: "Whatever you try to put on me will bounce back on you." That made him angry. He held up his hand to slap my face. I raised my fist. "Try it and I'll punch you in the nose." Realizing he couldn't scare me, he changed his tune and offered to be friends. "Here, have some wine." "Thanks," said I. "Here's some cheese.""

That is how Silent Samson, the Maccabee, saved Chelm. Whether or not he realized it, his gestures contained great truth. The people of the world belong to one family. Perhaps they will understand that one day, as the people of Chelm do.

In some ways they are not so foolish after all.

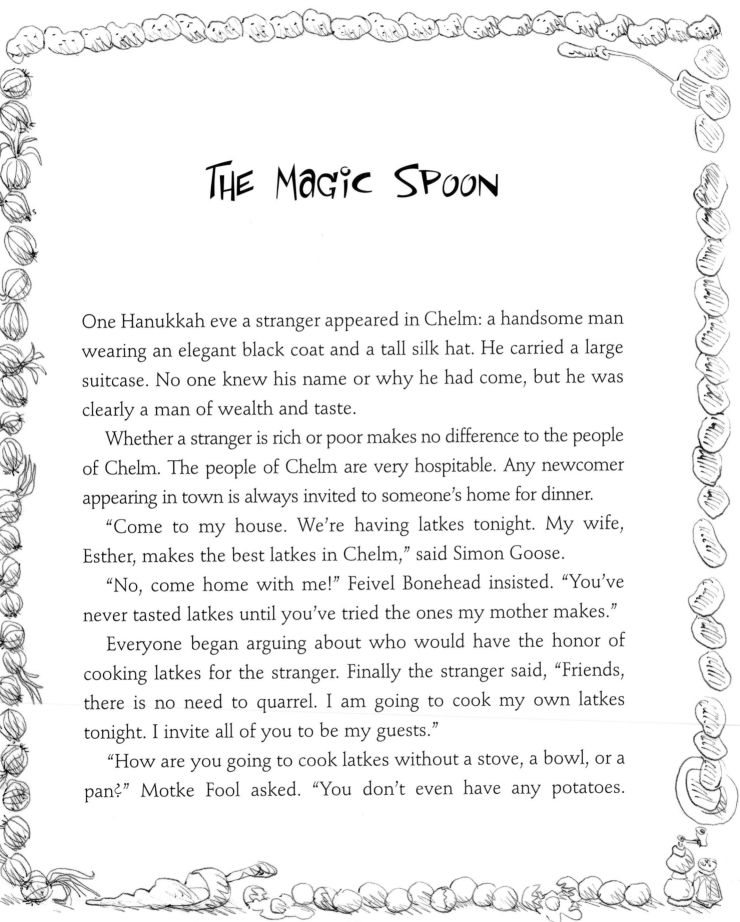

THE MAGIC SPOON

One Hanukkah eve a stranger appeared in Chelm: a handsome man wearing an elegant black coat and a tall silk hat. He carried a large suitcase. No one knew his name or why he had come, but he was clearly a man of wealth and taste.

Whether a stranger is rich or poor makes no difference to the people of Chelm. The people of Chelm are very hospitable. Any newcomer appearing in town is always invited to someone's home for dinner.

"Come to my house. We're having latkes tonight. My wife, Esther, makes the best latkes in Chelm," said Simon Goose.

"No, come home with me!" Feivel Bonehead insisted. "You've never tasted latkes until you've tried the ones my mother makes."

Everyone began arguing about who would have the honor of cooking latkes for the stranger. Finally the stranger said, "Friends, there is no need to quarrel. I am going to cook my own latkes tonight. I invite all of you to be my guests."

"How are you going to cook latkes without a stove, a bowl, or a pan?" Motke Fool asked. "You don't even have any potatoes.

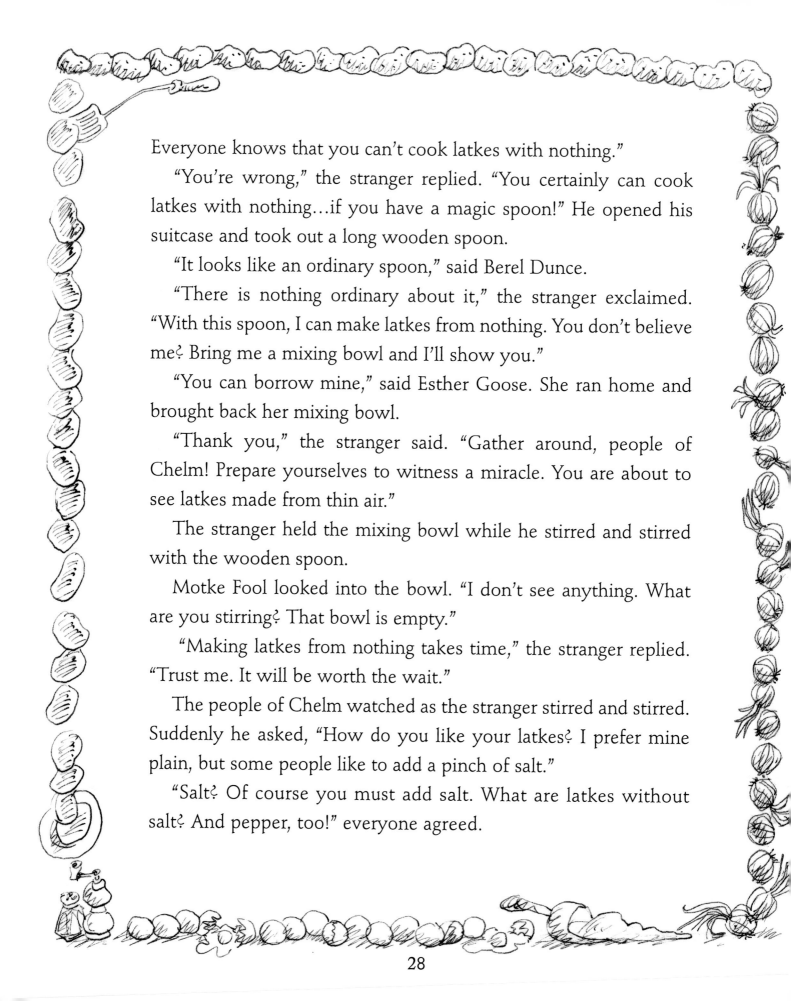

Everyone knows that you can't cook latkes with nothing."

"You're wrong," the stranger replied. "You certainly can cook latkes with nothing…if you have a magic spoon!" He opened his suitcase and took out a long wooden spoon.

"It looks like an ordinary spoon," said Berel Dunce.

"There is nothing ordinary about it," the stranger exclaimed. "With this spoon, I can make latkes from nothing. You don't believe me? Bring me a mixing bowl and I'll show you."

"You can borrow mine," said Esther Goose. She ran home and brought back her mixing bowl.

"Thank you," the stranger said. "Gather around, people of Chelm! Prepare yourselves to witness a miracle. You are about to see latkes made from thin air."

The stranger held the mixing bowl while he stirred and stirred with the wooden spoon.

Motke Fool looked into the bowl. "I don't see anything. What are you stirring? That bowl is empty."

"Making latkes from nothing takes time," the stranger replied. "Trust me. It will be worth the wait."

The people of Chelm watched as the stranger stirred and stirred. Suddenly he asked, "How do you like your latkes? I prefer mine plain, but some people like to add a pinch of salt."

"Salt? Of course you must add salt. What are latkes without salt? And pepper, too!" everyone agreed.

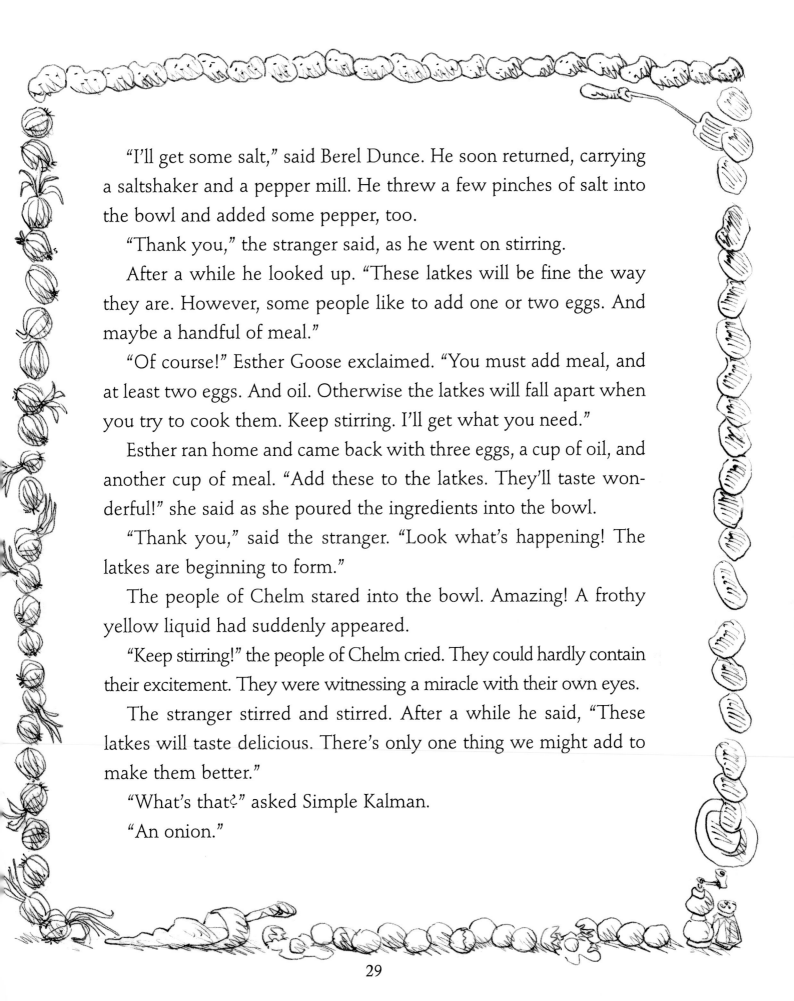

"I'll get some salt," said Berel Dunce. He soon returned, carrying a saltshaker and a pepper mill. He threw a few pinches of salt into the bowl and added some pepper, too.

"Thank you," the stranger said, as he went on stirring.

After a while he looked up. "These latkes will be fine the way they are. However, some people like to add one or two eggs. And maybe a handful of meal."

"Of course!" Esther Goose exclaimed. "You must add meal, and at least two eggs. And oil. Otherwise the latkes will fall apart when you try to cook them. Keep stirring. I'll get what you need."

Esther ran home and came back with three eggs, a cup of oil, and another cup of meal. "Add these to the latkes. They'll taste wonderful!" she said as she poured the ingredients into the bowl.

"Thank you," said the stranger. "Look what's happening! The latkes are beginning to form."

The people of Chelm stared into the bowl. Amazing! A frothy yellow liquid had suddenly appeared.

"Keep stirring!" the people of Chelm cried. They could hardly contain their excitement. They were witnessing a miracle with their own eyes.

The stranger stirred and stirred. After a while he said, "These latkes will taste delicious. There's only one thing we might add to make them better."

"What's that?" asked Simple Kalman.

"An onion."

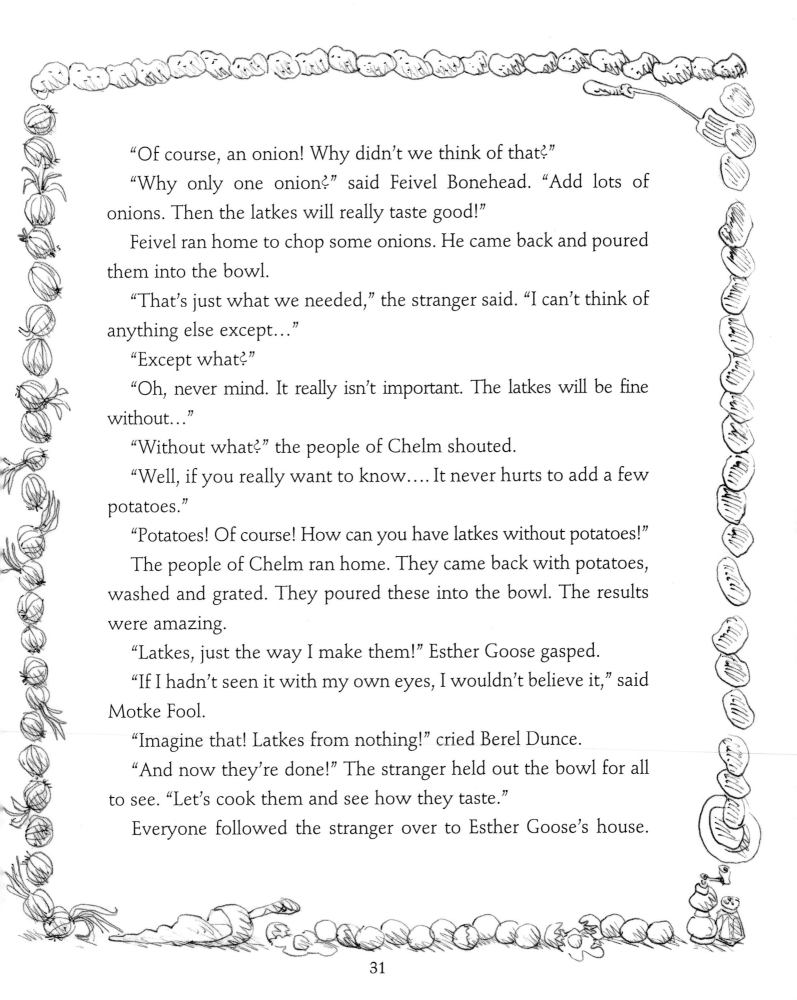

"Of course, an onion! Why didn't we think of that?"

"Why only one onion?" said Feivel Bonehead. "Add lots of onions. Then the latkes will really taste good!"

Feivel ran home to chop some onions. He came back and poured them into the bowl.

"That's just what we needed," the stranger said. "I can't think of anything else except…"

"Except what?"

"Oh, never mind. It really isn't important. The latkes will be fine without…"

"Without what?" the people of Chelm shouted.

"Well, if you really want to know…. It never hurts to add a few potatoes."

"Potatoes! Of course! How can you have latkes without potatoes!"

The people of Chelm ran home. They came back with potatoes, washed and grated. They poured these into the bowl. The results were amazing.

"Latkes, just the way I make them!" Esther Goose gasped.

"If I hadn't seen it with my own eyes, I wouldn't believe it," said Motke Fool.

"Imagine that! Latkes from nothing!" cried Berel Dunce.

"And now they're done!" The stranger held out the bowl for all to see. "Let's cook them and see how they taste."

Everyone followed the stranger over to Esther Goose's house.

Esther placed an iron pan on the stove. She poured in some oil. When it was hot, she added the latke mixture, a tablespoon at a time. The latkes began to cook. They filled the kitchen with their delicious smell.

"And to think this was all made from nothing," said Simple Kalman. He still couldn't believe it.

Soon the latkes were done. "Let's see how they taste," the stranger suggested.

They tasted delicious!

"These are the best latkes I ever ate," said Motke Fool.

"I never cooked better ones myself," said Esther Goose.

"It is truly a miracle. Latkes from nothing," said the rabbi.

The latkes disappeared in a flash. The people of Chelm demanded more, so the stranger mixed up batch after batch with his magic spoon. The people of Chelm provided the extra ingredients.

When all had eaten their fill, the stranger washed his magic spoon. He dried it with his handkerchief and put it back in his suitcase.

"Thank you for a lovely evening and a happy, happy Hanukkah," he said. "Now, if you will excuse me, I must be on my way."

"Where are you going? Stay here with us. Hanukkah's just begun. We can have latkes every night," said Berel Dunce.

The stranger shook his head. "No, I really must be off. My friends in Lublin are expecting me. I have to leave now. Otherwise I'll be late."

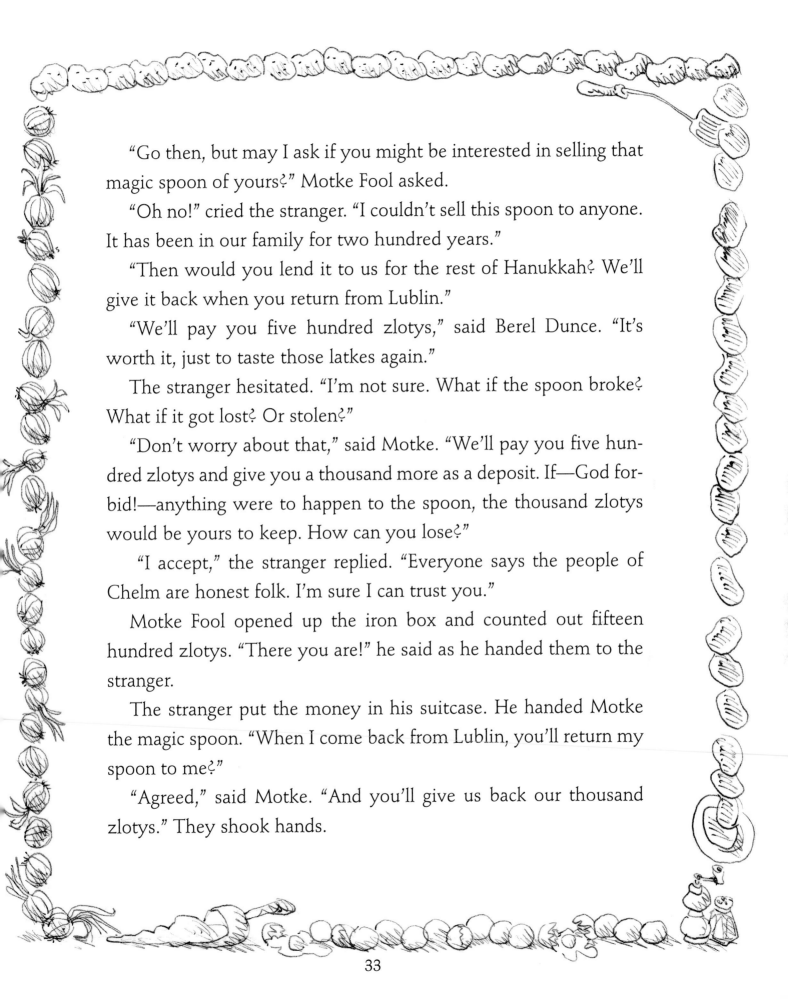

"Go then, but may I ask if you might be interested in selling that magic spoon of yours?" Motke Fool asked.

"Oh no!" cried the stranger. "I couldn't sell this spoon to anyone. It has been in our family for two hundred years."

"Then would you lend it to us for the rest of Hanukkah? We'll give it back when you return from Lublin."

"We'll pay you five hundred zlotys," said Berel Dunce. "It's worth it, just to taste those latkes again."

The stranger hesitated. "I'm not sure. What if the spoon broke? What if it got lost? Or stolen?"

"Don't worry about that," said Motke. "We'll pay you five hundred zlotys and give you a thousand more as a deposit. If—God forbid!—anything were to happen to the spoon, the thousand zlotys would be yours to keep. How can you lose?"

"I accept," the stranger replied. "Everyone says the people of Chelm are honest folk. I'm sure I can trust you."

Motke Fool opened up the iron box and counted out fifteen hundred zlotys. "There you are!" he said as he handed them to the stranger.

The stranger put the money in his suitcase. He handed Motke the magic spoon. "When I come back from Lublin, you'll return my spoon to me?"

"Agreed," said Motke. "And you'll give us back our thousand zlotys." They shook hands.

The stranger smiled. Without another word he tipped his hat, picked up his suitcase, and walked out of town.

The people of Chelm feasted every night for the rest of Hanukkah. They made piles and piles of latkes with the magic spoon. Of course they added some extra ingredients—salt, pepper, meal, oil, eggs, onions, and potatoes.

But, strange to say, the mysterious stranger never came back. When he still hadn't appeared a month after Hanukkah, the people of Chelm sent word to Lublin. Nobody there knew anything about him.

The people of Chelm waited the rest of that year, and the next, and the year after that. But the stranger never returned.

"As long as we have the magic spoon, we may as well use it," said Motke Fool. So every year they made heaps and heaps of latkes out of thin air, enough for the whole town.

"Do you think the stranger will ever come back?" Simon Goose asked as he spread applesauce and sour cream over his latkes.

"So what if he doesn't?" said Stupid Shmelke, finishing his fifth helping. "We still have the magic spoon. We can still make latkes from nothing. A secret like that is worth millions, and it only cost us fifteen hundred zlotys."

Together they laughed. "We got the best of that bargain!"

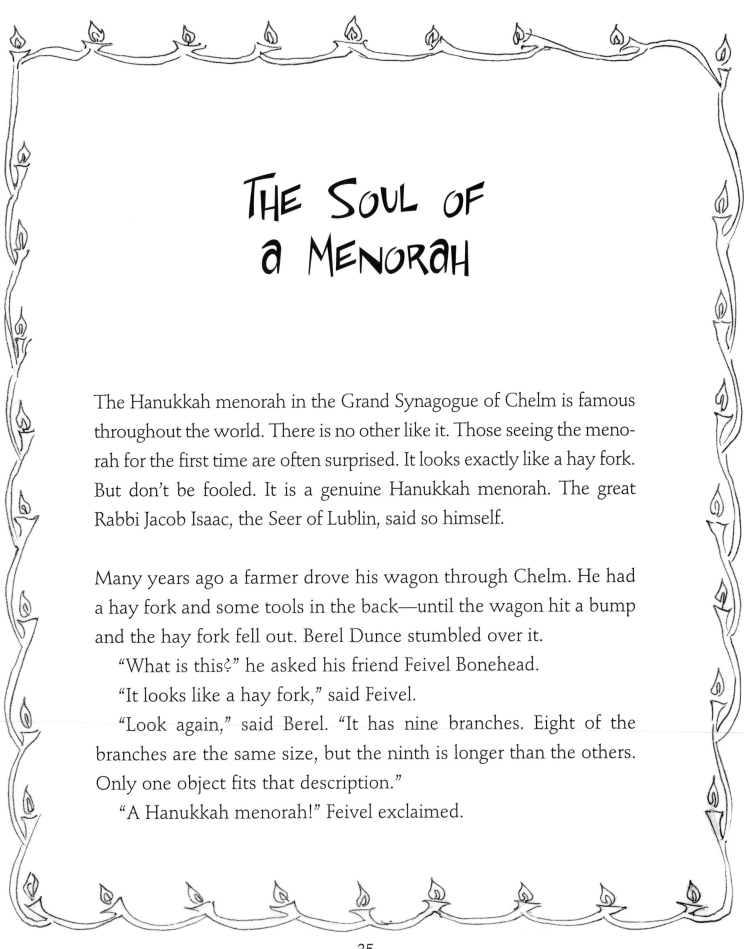

The Soul of a Menorah

The Hanukkah menorah in the Grand Synagogue of Chelm is famous throughout the world. There is no other like it. Those seeing the menorah for the first time are often surprised. It looks exactly like a hay fork. But don't be fooled. It is a genuine Hanukkah menorah. The great Rabbi Jacob Isaac, the Seer of Lublin, said so himself.

Many years ago a farmer drove his wagon through Chelm. He had a hay fork and some tools in the back—until the wagon hit a bump and the hay fork fell out. Berel Dunce stumbled over it.

"What is this?" he asked his friend Feivel Bonehead.

"It looks like a hay fork," said Feivel.

"Look again," said Berel. "It has nine branches. Eight of the branches are the same size, but the ninth is longer than the others. Only one object fits that description."

"A Hanukkah menorah!" Feivel exclaimed.

"This must be a Hanukkah menorah," Berel continued. "But how would a Hanukkah menorah come to be lying in the street?"

"Maybe it came down from heaven. Perhaps this menorah is a gift from God to us," said Feivel.

"We can't leave it here. Quick, Feivel! Let's clean up this menorah and take it to the synagogue where it belongs."

Berel and Feivel scraped the dirt off the hay fork and polished it until it shone. They oiled the wooden handle until it gleamed. Now the hay fork truly looked splendid. Berel and Feivel carried it to the synagogue.

"Why are you bringing a hay fork in here?" Bunam Ox shouted at Berel and Feivel. "I just mopped the floor. Take that hay fork back to the stable where it belongs."

"Look again, Bunam," Feivel and Berel said. "You've never seen a hay fork like this. It has nine branches—count them! One is taller than the rest. Only one object looks like that."

"A menorah!" Bunam gasped. "How did it get to Chelm?"

"We found it in the street. Feivel thinks God threw it down from heaven," Berel said.

"How else could it have gotten here?" Feivel asked.

"That doesn't matter," said Bunam. "What's important now is what we do with it. Right now we have to get this menorah ready. It will be dark soon. People will be coming to light the Hanukkah candles."

Bunam stuck the hay fork in a bucket of sand so it wouldn't fall over. Since it was the fifth night of Hanukkah, he took six thick candles and stuck them on the first six tines. The candle on the longer tine would serve as the shammes, to light the others.

When the men of Chelm gathered in the synagogue for evening prayers, they were surprised to see a hay fork standing in a bucket.

"Why is that hay fork here?" they asked.

"Open your eyes!" said Bunam Ox. "Can't you tell a menorah when you see one?"

"We found it in the street. God threw it down from heaven," Feivel and Berel added.

Word of the miraculous menorah spread through Chelm like fire through dry leaves. People from the surrounding countryside came streaming into town to see it. Among them was a farmer who had been searching all day for a missing hay fork.

"That's my hay fork!" he shouted as soon as he saw the menorah.

The people of Chelm were outraged. "Dolt! Mooncalf! Since when does a hay fork shine like silver? Did you ever see a hay fork lit with Hanukkah candles?"

"It's my hay fork, I tell you! I broke the handle once. I fixed it with a metal collar and two screws. Look! There they are!"

There were indeed a metal collar and two screws holding the wooden handle together. Was the farmer correct? What was this strange object?

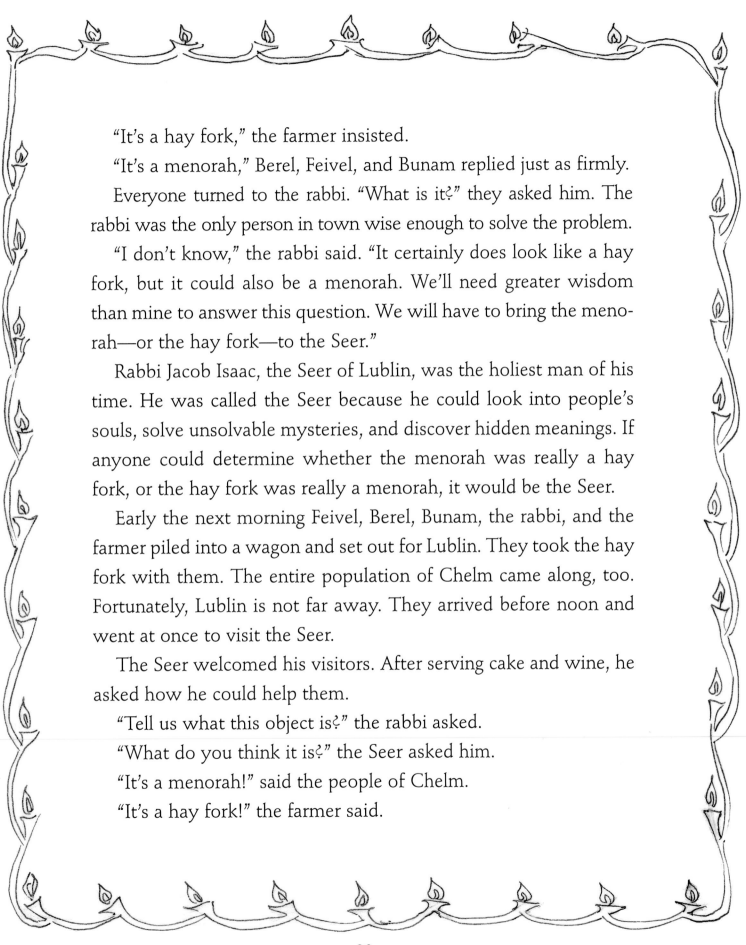

"It's a hay fork," the farmer insisted.

"It's a menorah," Berel, Feivel, and Bunam replied just as firmly.

Everyone turned to the rabbi. "What is it?" they asked him. The rabbi was the only person in town wise enough to solve the problem.

"I don't know," the rabbi said. "It certainly does look like a hay fork, but it could also be a menorah. We'll need greater wisdom than mine to answer this question. We will have to bring the menorah—or the hay fork—to the Seer."

Rabbi Jacob Isaac, the Seer of Lublin, was the holiest man of his time. He was called the Seer because he could look into people's souls, solve unsolvable mysteries, and discover hidden meanings. If anyone could determine whether the menorah was really a hay fork, or the hay fork was really a menorah, it would be the Seer.

Early the next morning Feivel, Berel, Bunam, the rabbi, and the farmer piled into a wagon and set out for Lublin. They took the hay fork with them. The entire population of Chelm came along, too. Fortunately, Lublin is not far away. They arrived before noon and went at once to visit the Seer.

The Seer welcomed his visitors. After serving cake and wine, he asked how he could help them.

"Tell us what this object is?" the rabbi asked.

"What do you think it is?" the Seer asked him.

"It's a menorah!" said the people of Chelm.

"It's a hay fork!" the farmer said.

The Seer stroked his beard. "This is not an easy question to answer. The object has nine branches. Eight are the same height, but one is taller than the others, so it could be a menorah. On the other hand, it does indeed look like a hay fork. There is only one way that I know to solve this problem. Our Master, the great rabbi and teacher Isaac Luria, of blessed memory, taught us not to be deceived by an object's outer appearance. We must always look inward to discover its hidden nature. Sparks of holiness can be found in the most common, ordinary things. A blind beggar singing in the marketplace might be an angel. An old boot may hold the key to a cosmic riddle. We must constantly search for these hidden sparks so that we can uncover their true holiness. I believe that is what happened in this case. The people of Chelm discovered the holy sparks hidden in a hay fork. They lifted them up by transforming the hay fork into a holy object, a menorah."

"That's right!" said Berel, Feivel, and Bunam.

The Seer continued. "Once holy sparks have been lifted, they cannot be lowered. This object might have been a hay fork in its earlier existence, but now it is a menorah. It must remain a menorah. It cannot be used as a hay fork again. That would be a sin."

"This is true," said the rabbi.

"But what about me?" cried the farmer. "I still need a hay fork."

"And you will have one," the Seer said. He turned to the people of Chelm. "The farmer has come here in good faith. He needs a hay

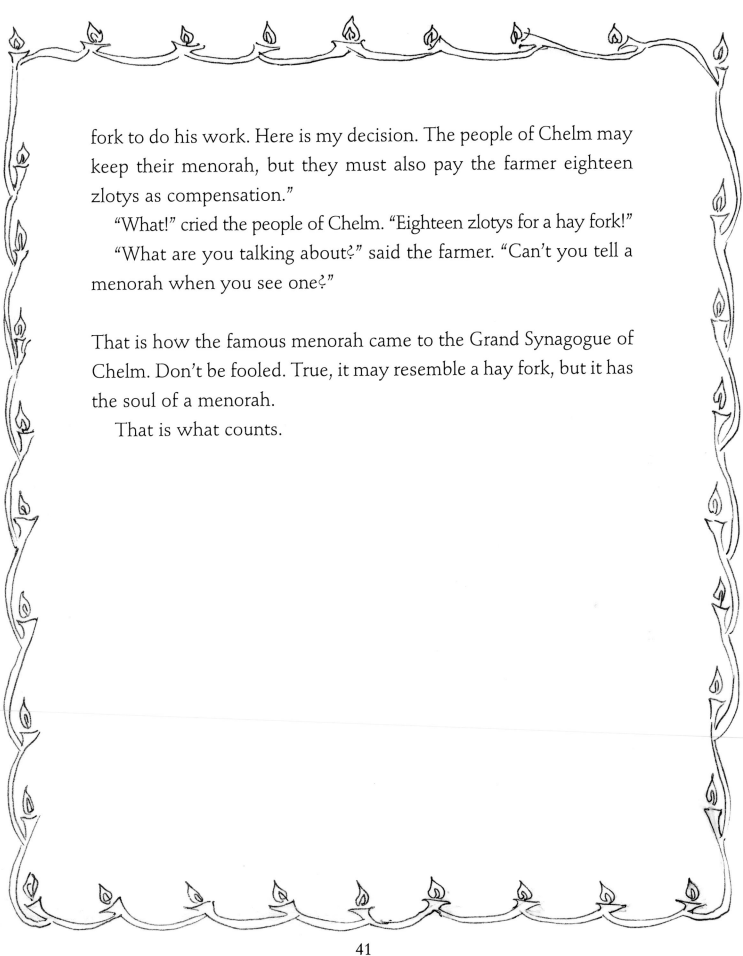

fork to do his work. Here is my decision. The people of Chelm may keep their menorah, but they must also pay the farmer eighteen zlotys as compensation."

"What!" cried the people of Chelm. "Eighteen zlotys for a hay fork!"

"What are you talking about?" said the farmer. "Can't you tell a menorah when you see one?"

That is how the famous menorah came to the Grand Synagogue of Chelm. Don't be fooled. True, it may resemble a hay fork, but it has the soul of a menorah.

That is what counts.

Wisdom for Sale

Prince Radziwill once paid a visit to Chelm. The people of Chelm welcomed him as an honored guest. Since the prince arrived during the Hanukkah season, they invited him to attend the lighting of the hay fork menorah in the Grand Synagogue. They let the prince examine the magic spoon and demonstrated how to make latkes from nothing. They presented him with a silver dreidel of the kind made only in Chelm.

The prince could not stop laughing. He laughed so hard his grooms had to help him into his carriage.

Just before leaving, he leaned out the window and said to the people of Chelm, "Thank you for a wonderful time. I can't remember when I laughed so hard. A hay fork menorah! Latkes made from nothing! A dreidel without any letters! Ha, ha, ha, ha, ha! You are the funniest people I ever met! What they say about Chelm is true.

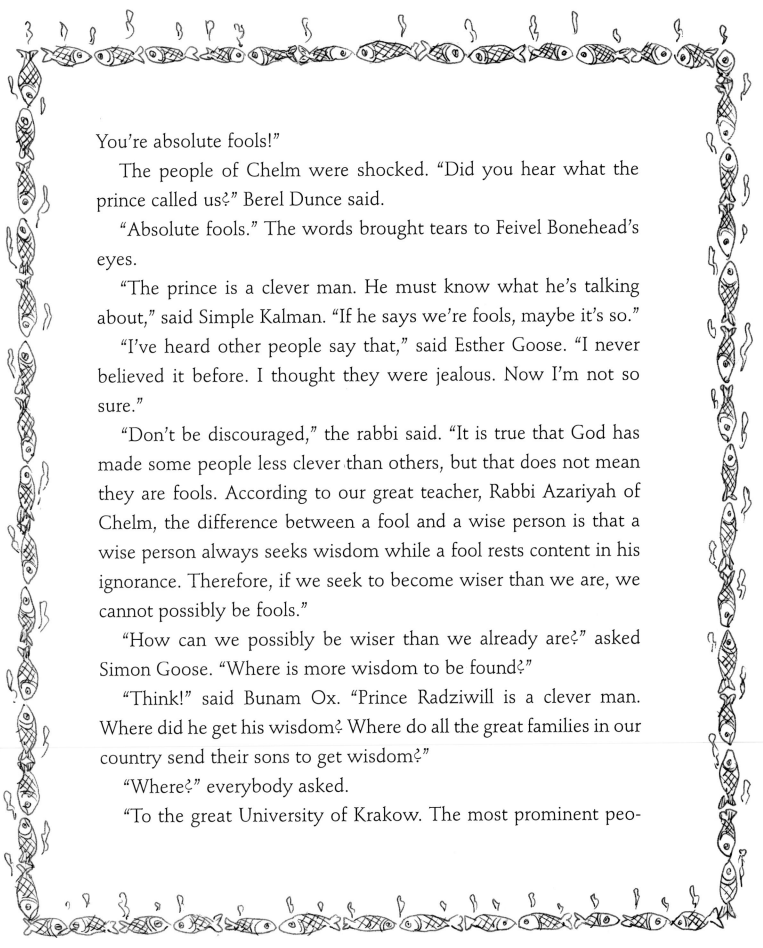

You're absolute fools!"

The people of Chelm were shocked. "Did you hear what the prince called us?" Berel Dunce said.

"Absolute fools." The words brought tears to Feivel Bonehead's eyes.

"The prince is a clever man. He must know what he's talking about," said Simple Kalman. "If he says we're fools, maybe it's so."

"I've heard other people say that," said Esther Goose. "I never believed it before. I thought they were jealous. Now I'm not so sure."

"Don't be discouraged," the rabbi said. "It is true that God has made some people less clever than others, but that does not mean they are fools. According to our great teacher, Rabbi Azariyah of Chelm, the difference between a fool and a wise person is that a wise person always seeks wisdom while a fool rests content in his ignorance. Therefore, if we seek to become wiser than we are, we cannot possibly be fools."

"How can we possibly be wiser than we already are?" asked Simon Goose. "Where is more wisdom to be found?"

"Think!" said Bunam Ox. "Prince Radziwill is a clever man. Where did he get his wisdom? Where do all the great families in our country send their sons to get wisdom?"

"Where?" everybody asked.

"To the great University of Krakow. The most prominent people in the land send their children there. Look at any great man in this country and you will find that he is a graduate of the University of Krakow."

"This university must be full of wisdom. It must be good wisdom, too, if rich folk are buying it," said Motke Fool.

"Maybe we can buy some, too," said Berel Dunce.

"I don't know," said Simple Kalman. "This wisdom probably costs a great deal of money. Only the rich can afford it."

"We have thirty thousand zlotys in the town treasury," said Feivel Bonehead. "Surely we can afford to buy some wisdom. Besides, the children of the rich are absolute fools. We've all seen them racing their horses over the countryside, drinking and gambling like wild men. It must require a lot of wisdom to turn them into sensible human beings. We won't need as much. We're already wise. We just want to become a little wiser, that's all."

"I have an idea," said Motke Fool. "Why don't we send a delegation to the University of Krakow to buy a sample of wisdom? We'll examine it. If we like it, we can buy more."

The people of Chelm decided that was a good idea. They voted to send Berel Dunce and Feivel Bonehead to Krakow with four hundred zlotys from the town treasury to purchase a sample of wisdom.

Krakow is nearly three hundred miles from Chelm. It took Berel and Feivel two weeks to get there. When they arrived, they asked two young gentlemen how to get to the University of Krakow.

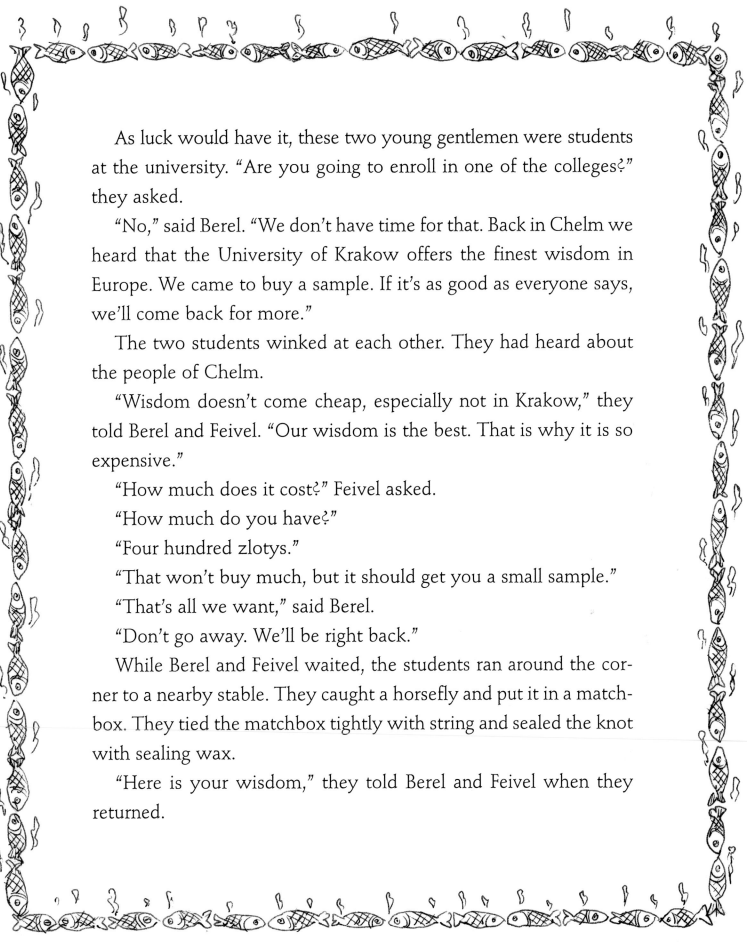

As luck would have it, these two young gentlemen were students at the university. "Are you going to enroll in one of the colleges?" they asked.

"No," said Berel. "We don't have time for that. Back in Chelm we heard that the University of Krakow offers the finest wisdom in Europe. We came to buy a sample. If it's as good as everyone says, we'll come back for more."

The two students winked at each other. They had heard about the people of Chelm.

"Wisdom doesn't come cheap, especially not in Krakow," they told Berel and Feivel. "Our wisdom is the best. That is why it is so expensive."

"How much does it cost?" Feivel asked.

"How much do you have?"

"Four hundred zlotys."

"That won't buy much, but it should get you a small sample."

"That's all we want," said Berel.

"Don't go away. We'll be right back."

While Berel and Feivel waited, the students ran around the corner to a nearby stable. They caught a horsefly and put it in a matchbox. They tied the matchbox tightly with string and sealed the knot with sealing wax.

"Here is your wisdom," they told Berel and Feivel when they returned.

"Is that all? Four hundred zlotys certainly doesn't buy much," Feivel said as he counted out the money.

"Trust me. You won't be disappointed," the first student replied.

"Don't open the box until you get to Chelm," the second student added.

Berel and Feivel promised not to look. They took the matchbox and started home.

"This must be good wisdom," Berel said to Feivel as they walked along. "Listen! I hear it buzzing. It's the same sound our rabbi makes when he studies the holy books. You know how wise he is!"

Feivel held the matchbox to his ear. "You're right! I can hear it, too. I wonder what this Krakow wisdom looks like."

"We promised not to open the box until we got to Chelm," Berel reminded him.

"What's the harm? A little peek can't hurt." Feivel broke the seal and unwound the string. He pushed open the matchbox. The horsefly flew out. It stung Feivel between the eyes. "Ow!" yelped Feivel. He smacked his forehead. That was the end of the horsefly, along with four hundred zlotys' worth of wisdom.

"Now you've done it! You've smashed our wisdom," said Berel.

"Very strange," said Feivel. "The wisdom of Krakow resembles a squashed horsefly. I never thought horseflies were particularly clever creatures. We have plenty of them in Chelm. Maybe the ones in Krakow are different."

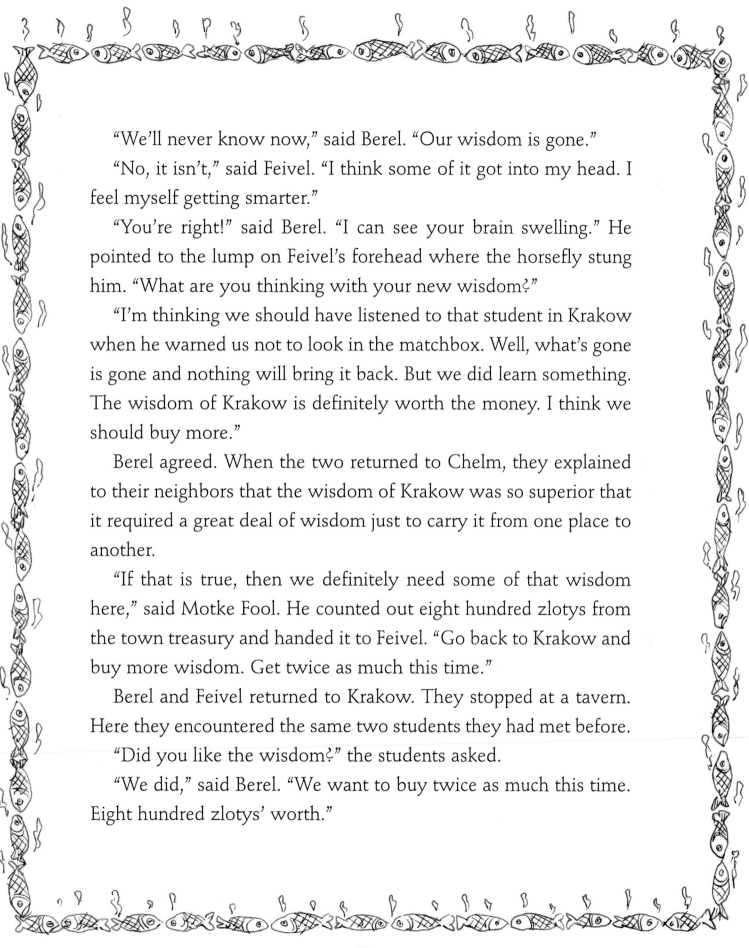

"We'll never know now," said Berel. "Our wisdom is gone."

"No, it isn't," said Feivel. "I think some of it got into my head. I feel myself getting smarter."

"You're right!" said Berel. "I can see your brain swelling." He pointed to the lump on Feivel's forehead where the horsefly stung him. "What are you thinking with your new wisdom?"

"I'm thinking we should have listened to that student in Krakow when he warned us not to look in the matchbox. Well, what's gone is gone and nothing will bring it back. But we did learn something. The wisdom of Krakow is definitely worth the money. I think we should buy more."

Berel agreed. When the two returned to Chelm, they explained to their neighbors that the wisdom of Krakow was so superior that it required a great deal of wisdom just to carry it from one place to another.

"If that is true, then we definitely need some of that wisdom here," said Motke Fool. He counted out eight hundred zlotys from the town treasury and handed it to Feivel. "Go back to Krakow and buy more wisdom. Get twice as much this time."

Berel and Feivel returned to Krakow. They stopped at a tavern. Here they encountered the same two students they had met before.

"Did you like the wisdom?" the students asked.

"We did," said Berel. "We want to buy twice as much this time. Eight hundred zlotys' worth."

The students' eyes opened wide when they saw the money. "We'll get some wisdom for you. The very best!"

The students caught a mouse and put it in a box with some grain and wool soaked with water. They tied the box with string and sealed it with sealing wax. Then back they went to the tavern.

"Here's your wisdom," they told Berel and Feivel.

Berel counted out the money while Feivel held the box to his ear. "This must be good wisdom," he said. "It squeaks, like the door to our rabbi's library. You know how much wisdom that library contains!"

"Remember, don't open the box until you get to Chelm," the students told them.

"You don't have to remind me. I know that," said Feivel, tapping his head. "I'm smarter now."

Berel and Feivel brought the box back to Chelm. Everyone gathered in the town hall to have a look at this new wisdom. Berel broke the seal. Feivel unwound the string. They handed the box to Motke Fool, who opened it.

A mouse jumped out. People screamed. They scrambled to get out of the way as the mouse streaked across the floor—straight into the jaws of the town hall cat.

The people of Chelm were outraged. "You wicked cat!" they screamed. "What right have you to take our wisdom? You didn't pay for it. Give it back! You can't keep all that wisdom for yourself!"

The cat ignored them. She began licking her paws.

"I'll get our wisdom back," said Simple Kalman. He tried to grab the cat. He might as well have tried to grab the wind. The cat slipped through his hands and ran out the door. The people of Chelm chased it around the town hall. The cat climbed the statue of Silent Samson and leaped onto the roof.

"What do we do now?" the people of Chelm asked.

"Leave it to me," said Feivel. "That cat thinks she's smart because she's full of wisdom. Well, I have some wisdom, too. I know how to get her down."

"How?"

"Set fire to the building. She'll come down as soon as she sees the flames."

"Feivel is right!" the people of Chelm exclaimed. They lit torches and set fire to the town hall. The building was ablaze within minutes. Feivel proved correct. The cat leaped onto the bakery roof.

"What will we do?" the people of Chelm asked.

"Burn the bakery," said Feivel.

The people of Chelm set fire to the bakery. The cat leaped to the roof of the butcher shop. The people of Chelm set fire to the butcher shop. The cat leaped to the roof of Simple Kalman's house.

"Burn it!" said Feivel, again and again.

The cat leaped from roof to roof until she reached the edge of town. She jumped to the ground and ran into a field. The people of

Chelm didn't have the strength to chase her. By then the whole town was ablaze.

"What went wrong?" the people of Chelm asked Feivel.

Feivel sighed. "I made a mistake. I should have known from the beginning that I could never outsmart that cat. After all, I have only four hundred zlotys' worth of wisdom. The cat has twice as much. She must be the cleverest cat in the world. No wonder she made fools of us."

"Never mind. All is not lost," said Motke Fool. "The wisdom of Krakow has proven its value. We have seen a cat outsmart a whole town with just eight hundred zlotys' worth. I say we use whatever money is left in our treasury to buy wisdom. Let's send Berel and Feivel back to Krakow to buy enough for everyone. This time we'll know how to handle it. We'll all be geniuses. Chelm will be the most famous town in Europe. People will come from London, Paris, Rome—even Krakow—to learn from us!"

"Yes, yes!" everyone cried. "Buy wisdom! Chelm will be famous! Hurrah for Chelm!"

Berel and Feivel took the twenty-eight thousand eight hundred zlotys left in the town treasury and went back to Krakow. This time they traveled in a wagon, for they intended to buy a lot of wisdom, more than two men could carry. They had hardly arrived in the city when they ran into the same two students.

"You're back," they said. "Did you come for more wisdom?"

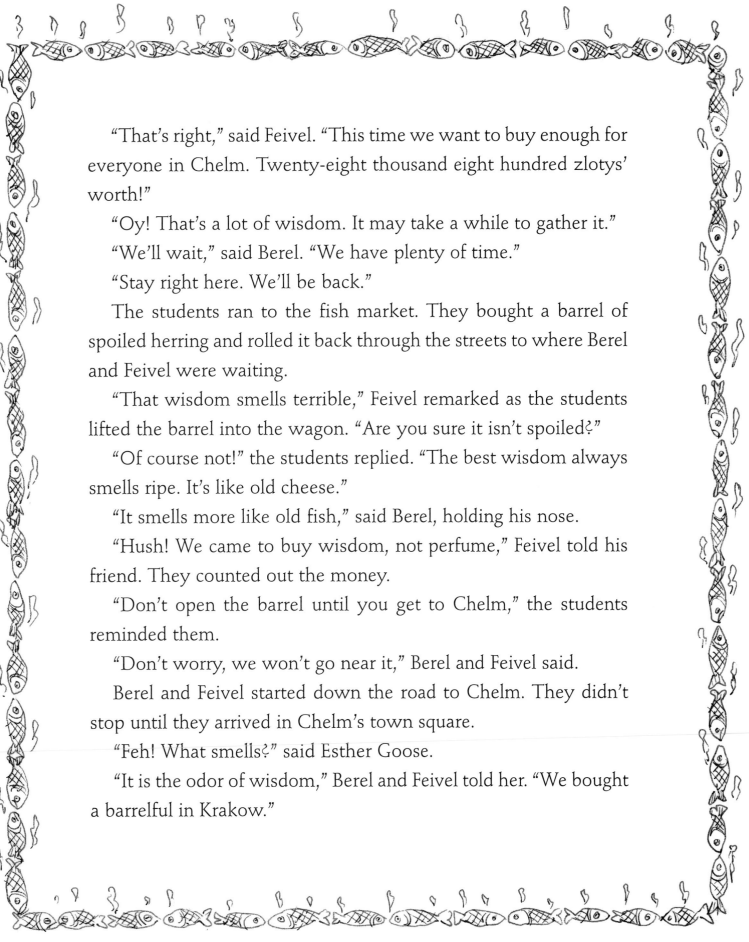

"That's right," said Feivel. "This time we want to buy enough for everyone in Chelm. Twenty-eight thousand eight hundred zlotys' worth!"

"Oy! That's a lot of wisdom. It may take a while to gather it."

"We'll wait," said Berel. "We have plenty of time."

"Stay right here. We'll be back."

The students ran to the fish market. They bought a barrel of spoiled herring and rolled it back through the streets to where Berel and Feivel were waiting.

"That wisdom smells terrible," Feivel remarked as the students lifted the barrel into the wagon. "Are you sure it isn't spoiled?"

"Of course not!" the students replied. "The best wisdom always smells ripe. It's like old cheese."

"It smells more like old fish," said Berel, holding his nose.

"Hush! We came to buy wisdom, not perfume," Feivel told his friend. They counted out the money.

"Don't open the barrel until you get to Chelm," the students reminded them.

"Don't worry, we won't go near it," Berel and Feivel said.

Berel and Feivel started down the road to Chelm. They didn't stop until they arrived in Chelm's town square.

"Feh! What smells?" said Esther Goose.

"It is the odor of wisdom," Berel and Feivel told her. "We bought a barrelful in Krakow."

"I thought wisdom was supposed to smell sweet," said Stupid Shmelke.

"Only to the wise," the rabbi explained. "As our great teacher, Rabbi Azariyah of Chelm, wrote, 'The smell of wisdom is a sweet savor to the wise, but a stench to fools.'"

"That barrel really smells bad. It must mean that we are really stupid," said Simple Kalman.

"But not for long!" Berel and Feivel exclaimed. "There's enough wisdom in this barrel for everybody in Chelm. As soon as we taste it, we'll all be wise. The barrel will smell sweeter than perfume."

The people of Chelm handed the barrel down from the wagon. They could hardly wait to be wise, if for no other reason than to get rid of that terrible smell. Bunam Ox pried open the barrel. He stuck in his head, took a deep breath, and fainted. If Berel and Feivel hadn't caught him, he would have fallen headfirst into the barrel.

"Are you wiser now?" everyone asked after he recovered his senses.

"I don't think so," said Bunam. "I must be getting stupider. That barrel smells worse than before."

"Something is wrong," the rabbi said. He pulled a piece of wisdom from the barrel and tasted it. "Feh!" he cried, spitting it out. "This wisdom tastes like rotten herring!"

"It smells like rotten herring!"

"It is rotten herring!"

The people of Chelm were furious. "Twenty-eight thousand eight hundred zlotys for a barrel of rotten herring!"

"We were cheated! It's Feivel's fault. Berel's, too!"

"Throw them in jail!"

"Tie them to the whipping post!"

"Run them out of town!"

"Now, wait!" the rabbi said. "Berel and Feivel are not guilty. We sent them to Krakow to buy wisdom, and they did. Aren't we wiser now? Haven't we all learned a great lesson?"

"Did we?"

"Of course we did. Listen, and I will explain."

The people of Chelm gathered around to hear the rabbi's words.

"Before we opened that barrel, we were fools. We couldn't tell a barrel of wisdom from a barrel of rotten herring. Now we can. Before we didn't know those rascals in Krakow were cheating us. Now we do. Before we thought the wisdom of Chelm was worthless compared to the wisdom of strangers. Now we know the value of our own true wisdom, the wisdom that God Himself sent down from heaven at the time of Creation. Compared to the wisdom of Chelm, the wisdom of the rest of the world is nothing but a barrel of rotten fish."

"But why did Prince Radziwill laugh at us?"

"Think! Where did Prince Radziwill go to school? He went to the

University of Krakow. The poor man's brain is stuffed with rotten herring, and he calls it wisdom. No wonder he laughed at us. If a person who cannot hear sees people dancing, he laughs at them, too. He thinks they are fools to leap and jump about so. But they are not fools. He cannot hear the music. But they can. And so can we!"

The barrel of rotten herring was rolled to the town dump. A new Chelm arose on the ashes of the old.

Nowhere in the world is Hanukkah celebrated with greater joy. The hay fork menorah is lit; delicious latkes are made from nothing with the magic spoon; dreidels without letters spin.

And the people of Chelm dance night and day to music that they alone can hear.

Author's Note

The real city of Chelm is located in eastern Poland, approximately forty kilometers from the border with Ukraine. However, the Chelm of Jewish legend can be anywhere in Eastern Europe. Chelm is the traditional town of fools. However, the people of Chelm are not stupid. Their reasoning is precise and their arguments are inspired. Unfortunately, they are nearly always wrong.

Some stories in this collection, such as "The Jar of Fools" and "Silent Samson, the Maccabee," are retellings of traditional Yiddish tales. Others, like "Sweeter than Honey, Purer than Oil," "The Knight of the Golden Slippers," and "The Magic Spoon," are adaptations of stories from other traditions. Still others, such as "How They Play Dreidel in Chelm," "The Soul of a Menorah," and "Wisdom for Sale" are original, although the episode with the cat is an old Chelm story. Writing a good Chelm story is a challenge. You almost have to think like a Chelmer to do it.